Willie Was Different

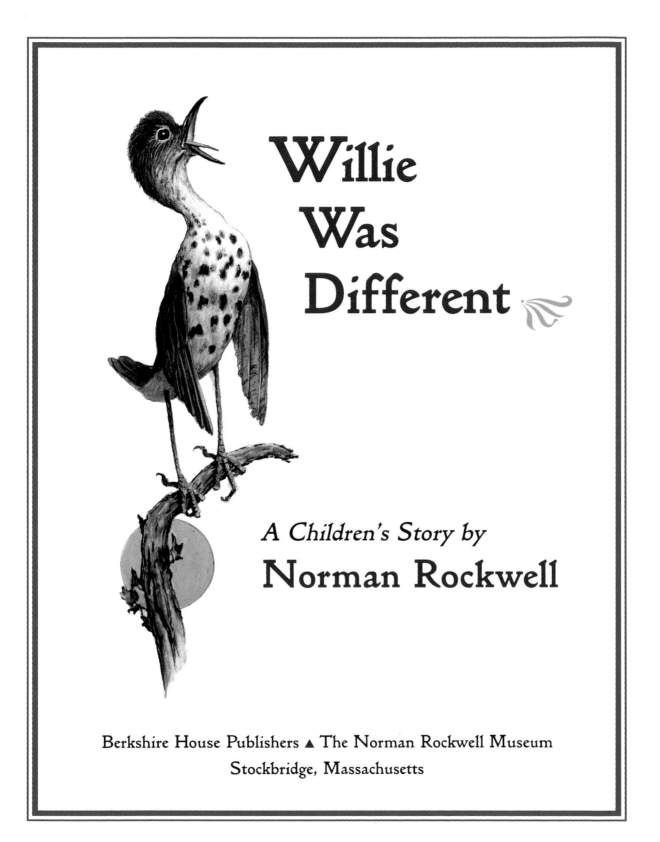

Willie
Was
Different

A Children's Story by
Norman Rockwell

Berkshire House Publishers ▲ The Norman Rockwell Museum
Stockbridge, Massachusetts

Berkshire House Publishers
PO Box 297
Stockbridge, Massachusetts 01262

▲

The Norman Rockwell Museum
Stockbridge, Massachusetts 01262

Library of Congress Cataloging-in-Publication Data

Rockwell, Norman, 1894–1978.
    Willie was different / written and illustrated by Norman Rockwell.
        p.   cm.
    Summary: Realizing that he is different from other wood thrushes, Willie
sets out on his own and becomes famous when he creates his own songs to
accompany a flautist who is his devoted friend.
    ISBN 0-936399-61-9
    [1. Wood thrush—Fiction. 2. Individuality—Fiction. 3. Fame—Fiction.]
I. Title.
    PZ7.R59487Wi   1994
    [Fic]—dc20   94-8785
                                                                                CIP
                                                                                AC

ISBN 0-936399-61-9

Book Design by Chris Hammill Paul

Printed in Singapore

10 9 8 7 6

Foreword ❧

We hope you will enjoy *Willie Was Different* as a story of the trials of genius and the satisfactions of true friendship. It demonstrates that Norman Rockwell's love of storytelling could be expressed in writing as well as in painting.

Although *Willie Was Different* stands on its own as a story, it has some other interesting qualities, too. First, Rockwell's many surviving friends are unanimous that *Willie Was Different* was an autobiographical sketch. Rockwell drew Willie as a spindly, pigeon-toed character with unruly red hair, just as he sometimes portrayed himself in amusing, self-deprecatory sketches. Read *My Adventures as an Illustrator*, Rockwell's own life story, to get a fuller flavor of the autobiographical character of *Willie Was Different*. Whether Miss Polly was modeled on Molly Punderson Rockwell, his third wife, and father and mother thrush on his own parents are questions his friends still debate with interest.

This both is and is not the story's first publication. Rockwell wrote the story and offered it to *McCall's* Magazine. He then did the color illustrations and *Willie Was Different* was published by *McCall's* in 1967. Rockwell seems to have intended his manuscript as an outline rather than as a finished text and he did not object to the many changes *McCall's* made in it. A year or so later, Molly Rockwell re-wrote the story extensively and Rockwell did the black and white illustrations to provide pictorial continuity for the expanded text. That version was published as a book for adult or advanced adolescent readers by Funk & Wagnalls in 1969.

This edition returns to Rockwell's original conception and as nearly as possible to his own manuscript, which it can fairly be said has never been published before. Though perhaps more like a working sketch than a finished work, Rockwell's original text has a clarity of expression, a mastery of narration, and an eye for telling detail reminiscent of his painting style. In this "original" version, *Willie Was Different* is once again clearly a children's story, albeit one with great appeal to sensitive adults as well.

There are a number of true touches in the illustrations of the book. All of the figures in the "top-hat" illustration on page 22 were drawn from real ornithological personalities of the time. Rockwell also included himself in a number of the illustrations. There is a "young" Norman Rockwell on pages 18 and 31, and an "older" Rockwell, disguised by a balding head, also on page 18. He modeled for several other figures as well, but gave them different faces. Molly Rockwell posed for several of the Miss Polly pictures, but Miss Polly's face was not drawn from hers.

Sad to say, *Willie Was Different* is not a true story. Although Rockwell wrote it as if it were a narration of true events, there is no record of a thrush like Willie, either in the Stockbridge newspapers of the time or in the archives of the Ornithological Section of the Smithsonian Institution. Visitors there can hear wonderful bird songs, and perhaps none more beautiful than the song of the wood thrush, but there are no thrush cadenzas. The Willie Room, and Willie's fame, exist entirely in the pages of this book.

Willie was a wood thrush. In his thrush family he had a strict, proud father, a loving mother, and two rowdy older brothers named George and Albert.

Willie was different. He felt and looked different. He was gawky and pigeon-toed. Maybe way down deep inside himself he felt he was a genius.

Willie's father was always preaching about
the fine qualities of the wood thrush.
"A wood thrush," he would say, "is not
mighty like an eagle. Or beautiful like a
peacock. Or wise like an owl. Certainly
wood thrushes do not try to talk like
humans, as parrots do. Nor do they sing
like nightingales. No! We have a simple song
that has never changed through the ages!"

Willie's father would say, "It is only six
notes long, but it is perfect, and it is glorious.
Many famous human composers, such as
Handel, Weber, and Gounod, have been
inspired by our song."

Willie was proud of being a wood thrush.
But he also wanted to be himself. He was
tired of his father's daily lectures and of
trying to be like every other wood thrush.
Finally, he just couldn't stand it anymore.
So he flew away to a neighboring wood and
made himself a new home, alone.

Willie's mother was concerned for him. She came to see him and made sure he was getting enough berries, spiders, worms, seeds, and wild fruits to eat, but she didn't try to convince him to return home. She was wise enough to let him live as he needed to live.

Willie was happy by himself in the woods. He flew about from birch to oak to pine tree and watched the sun rise and set, and wondered what his genius would be. Then one twilight, Willie heard the sweet notes of a flute. He flew closer to listen better.

Miss Polly, the town librarian, was playing her flute at an open window. She was playing a song by Handel which included the thrush's call.

Filled with joy to hear the thrush song from the flute, Willie began to sing along with it. At first he sang just the simple song of the thrush. Then he added cadenzas and trills inspired by his own moods. Willie realized his destiny! He must become a great, great singer!

Miss Polly had never been accompanied by a bird before, but she found Willie's music enchanting. She happily played duets with Willie until night fell and the moon rose.

The next morning, Miss Polly walked through the woods until she heard Willie, practicing his songs in a tree. She took notes and that evening, at the regular meeting of the Bird Watcher's Society, reported the amazing news of Willie, the creative thrush.

The bird watchers were flabbergasted. A thrush who composed his own music! No one had ever heard of such a thing! Could it possibly be true? They called up the experts at the National Ornithological Society in Washington, D.C.

The experts were flabbergasted, too, even if they wouldn't admit it.

And that very night, a motorcade of ornithological officials in top hats arrived at Miss Polly's house to see and hear the miraculous Willie.

It was true! Willie, full of pride and genius, sang his songs, though he didn't know what to make of all the people peering at him, snapping photographs, taking notes. Miss Polly urged him to sing again and again. Inspired, he sang more beautifully than ever before.

His audience fell silent. Willie *was* a genius! They knew it, and Willie knew it, too.

But later, as Willie rested in the dim top of a pine tree and Miss Polly served tea, the ornithologists told Miss Polly that Willie was too important a bird to stay out in the wilds. He must come to Washington and live in the aviary there. All the world deserved a chance to see and hear this remarkable creature.

Miss Polly worried. The aviary would be so different from the woods behind her house. But she felt a duty to Willie's genius, so she took him on the train to Washington.

Miss Polly was right. Away from his quiet wood and surrounded now by hundreds of strange birds, Willie couldn't sleep or eat or fly. Worse still, he couldn't sing.

Not even the sound of Miss Polly's flute
could cheer him or coax a note out of him.
Willie was proud to be different, to be a
genius, but he did not want to be a celebrity.

After a few days, Miss Polly put her foot down. She took Willie back home and returned him to his woods and meadows.

For quite a while, Willie kept to himself. But then, hearing the sweet sounds of Miss Polly's flute among the trees, he began to try his songs again. Very softly, just for themselves, Willie and Miss Polly, his true old friend, brought to life the songs they had created together.

The rest of the world did not forget Willie. The Ornithological Society built a shrine called "Willie's Room" in their museum. Even now, if you have the right spirit, you can find it among all the hustle and bustle, the honking horns and blaring radios of Washington, and going in, you can hear for yourself the miracle of Willie's genius, his music.

For that, as we know, was what made
Willie different.